ROAD WORK AHEAD

by **Anastasia Suen**

illustrated by **Jannie Ho**

VIKING
An Imprint of Penguin Group (USA) Inc.

VIKING
Published by Penguin Group
Penguin Young Readers Group, 345 Hudson Street, New York, New York 10014, U.S.A.
Penguin Group (Canada), 90 Eglinton Avenue East, Suite 700, Toronto, Ontario, Canada
M4P 2Y3 (a division of Pearson Penguin Canada Inc.)
Penguin Books Ltd, 80 Strand, London WC2R 0RL, England
Penguin Ireland, 25 St Stephen's Green, Dublin 2, Ireland (a division of Penguin Books Ltd)
Penguin Group (Australia), 250 Camberwell Road, Camberwell, Victoria 3124, Australia
(a division of Pearson Australia Group Pty Ltd)
Penguin Books India Pvt Ltd, 11 Community Centre, Panchsheel Park,
New Delhi – 110 017, India
Penguin Group (NZ), 67 Apollo Drive, Rosedale, Auckland 0632, New Zealand
(a division of Pearson New Zealand Ltd.)
Penguin Books (South Africa) (Pty) Ltd, 24 Sturdee Avenue, Rosebank, Johannesburg 2196,
South Africa

Penguin Books Ltd, Registered Offices: 80 Strand, London WC2R 0RL, England

First published in 2011 by Viking, a division of Penguin Young Readers Group

1   3   5   7   9   10   8   6   4   2

LIBRARY OF CONGRESS CATALOGING-IN-PUBLICATION DATA
Suen, Anastasia.
Roadwork ahead / by Anastasia Suen ; illustrated by Jannie Ho.
p. cm.
Summary: On the drive to Grandma's house, a boy and his mother
encounter work crews using machinery and tools to perform roadwork.
ISBN 978-0-670-01288-6 (hardcover)
Special Markets ISBN 978-0-670-78486-8 Not for resale
[1. Stories in rhyme. 2. Roads—Maintenance and repair—Fiction.]
I. Ho, Jannie, ill. II. Title.
PZ8.3.S9354Ro 2011
[E]—dc22
2011004545

Manufactured in China
Set in Memphis   Book design by Jim Hoover

This Imagination Library edition is published by Penguin Group (USA), a Pearson
company, exclusively for Dolly Parton's Imagination Library, a not-for-profit
program designed to inspire a love of reading and learning, sponsored in part by The
Dollywood Foundation. Penguin's trade editions of this work are available wherever
books are sold.

For Gloria, Louise, and Claire
—A.S.

To Mela, the best agent ever
—J.H.

Hello, Grandma, here we come!
You're making oatmeal cookies? Yum!

Road work ahead.

Move over. Go slow.

Jackhammers crack.

Look at them go.

People working above
trim bushes and trees.

They put up lights
so you can see.

Crew working below
use umbrellas and hose.

How do they know
where everything goes?

Trucks crossing,
one, two, three . . .

Look up ahead.
What do you see?

Left lane closed
for drilling holes.

Watch out now,
they're putting up poles.

Right lane closed
to pour concrete.

Workers plant trees
along the street.

SOFT ICE CREAM

People at work
here and there,

fixing things up
everywhere.

We're here at last. We made it through.
Oatmeal cookies for me and you!